Becky
the Best Friend
Fairy

31190

For Matilda, who knows the meaning of friendship

ORCHARD BOOKS

First published in Great Britain in 2016 by The Watts Publishing Group
This edition published in 2016 by The Watts Publishing Group

1 3 5 7 9 10 8 6 4 2

© 2016 Rainbow Magic Limited.
© 2016 HIT Entertainment Limited.
Illustrations © Orchard Books 2016

HiT entertainment

A CIP catalogue record for this book is available from the British Library.

ISBN 978 1 40834 056 1

Printed in Great Britain

MIX
Paper from
responsible sources
FSC® C104740
FSC
www.fsc.org

The paper and board used in this book are made from wood from responsible sources

Orchard Books
An imprint of Hachette Children's Group
Part of The Watts Publishing Group Limited
Carmelite House, 50 Victoria Embankment, London EC4Y 0DZ

An Hachette UK Company
www.hachette.co.uk
www.hachettechildrens.co.uk

The Strength of Friendship

Becky fluttered into the air and clapped her hands together, delighted that the girls were going to help her.

"One of my friends overheard Jack Frost talking to his goblins," she said. "He was sending some of his goblins here to the human world to bury my trinket box. Without it, best friends everywhere will start having silly arguments and falling out."

Rachel and Kirsty exchanged a glance.

"That's just happened to us," said Rachel. "It's already affecting friendships, Becky. We have to find it quickly!"

"But where shall we start looking?" asked Kirsty.

She stared out over the beach, thinking hard. Suddenly she realised that she was looking at a group of boys digging in the sand. They were

jostling and pushing each other, and two of them were flinging sand at the others.

"I wonder if they've been affected too," she said. "They don't look very friendly."

Just then, one of the boys looked around. Rachel gave a cry of surprise.

"Goblins!" she exclaimed. "They're goblins!"

"They must be burying the trinket box!" cried Kirsty. "We have to stop them. Come on!"

Becky swooped into Rachel's pocket and the girls scrambled down the dunes to the beach. They ran towards the goblins, but it was difficult to run fast on the soft sand.
One of the goblins looked up and gave a yell.

"Humans alert! Run for it!"

They kicked the sand over whatever they had been digging and darted away towards the rock pools. Each of them was carrying a bucket and a spade, and they were all making a terrific clanking, clanging noise.

"We have to follow them," said Rachel, panting.

Kirsty had stopped beside the place where the goblins had been digging.

"No, let's dig here," she said. "We should find out what they were burying – it might be the trinket box."

"They wouldn't have buried it here," Rachel argued. "They're sure to have it with them."

"But Jack Frost told them to bury it," said Kirsty, folding her arms. "I say we should dig here."

"No!" said Rachel, also folding her arms.

"Stop!" cried Becky, flying out of Rachel's pocket. "You're only arguing because the trinket box is missing."

The girls stared at her. They knew that she was right, but it was hard to feel as happy as usual. Something seemed different.

"You have to trust me," said Becky. "Both of you are right, but we need to follow the goblins first because they are moving fast. If they don't have the trinket box, we can come back here and dig for it. Don't let Jack Frost's tricks come between you!"

Rachel and Kirsty held out their hands to each other, and suddenly their cross feelings melted away.

"We'll never do that," said Kirsty. "You're right, we should follow the goblins first."

Still hand in hand, they raced towards the rock pools with Becky darting along beside them. They had to reach the goblins and find out if they still had the trinket box!

Rachel's Trick

Rachel and Kirsty kicked off their shoes and stepped carefully onto the rocks. They made their way around a large boulder and stopped. Six goblins were capering in the little rock pools, splashing water everywhere. Little crabs and sea creatures scuttled left and right.

"Stop!" cried Kirsty. "You're scaring the little sea creatures!"

"Who cares?" shouted one of the goblins. "Leave us alone!"

"You shouldn't jump in rock pools," said Rachel.

But the goblins just laughed and carried on. Kirsty stared at them, wondering how they could be stopped.

Then she noticed something odd. One
of the goblins was holding his bucket
very close to his
chest. The others had
all dropped their
buckets – or thrown
them at each other.
But the spottiest
goblin was behaving
as if his bucket was
made of gold.

Kirsty pulled herself up
onto a boulder and looked down into
the bucket. It was hard to see because the
goblin would not stop leaping around,
but she caught a glimpse of a small pink
box inside the bucket.

Feeling excited, she beckoned to Becky,
who fluttered up beside her.

"Is your trinket box pink?" she asked.

Becky nodded, and Kirsty pointed to the goblin still holding his bucket.

"I think he's got it," she said. "There's something pink inside his bucket – I bet it's your trinket box!"

Rachel had scrambled up to join them, and she clapped her hands together in delight when she heard the news. But Becky didn't look so thrilled.

"It's great that we've found it," she said. "But however are we going to get it back? That goblin is guarding it too well."

Rachel looked down at the rock pools, and suddenly an idea popped into her head.

"They're already interested in the rock pools," she said. "We just have to make them even more exciting. We might even be able to stop them scaring the sea creatures."

"How?" Becky asked.

"There are six goblins," said Rachel. "Can you magic up six fishing nets?"

Becky gave a flick of her wand, and instantly six green fishing nets on long sticks appeared in Rachel's hands. She slid down from the boulder and waved at the goblins.

"I've got something for you," she called.
"Don't run off – it's a present."

"Ooh, a present!" squealed several of
the goblins. "Give it! Give it!"

But the spottiest goblin held up a long-
fingered hand.

"Hold on a minute," he said, looking
suspicious. "Why would a pesky human
like you want to give *us* a present?
I don't trust you."

"I want you to stop jumping in the rock pools," said Rachel truthfully, holding up the nets. "With these, you can fish in the rock pools instead of jumping in them," she said. "You could even collect crabs and pretty shells in your buckets."

Each goblin ran up to snatch a net from her hand. The spottiest goblin was last. He grabbed the net, looked down at his bucket and scowled.

"What's the point of fishing when I don't have any room in my bucket?" he grumbled. "I can't fit anything else in there."

Rachel peered into the bucket. The trinket box completely filled it up. She tried to hide her excitement.

"That's easy," she said. "All you have to do is empty your bucket."

The goblin narrowed his eyes.

"Why are you trying to help me?" he asked.

"Because I don't want you to scare any more little crabs," said Rachel, pointing to a little rocky ledge behind him.

"Look, that's a good place to keep things safe. You could empty the things out of your bucket onto there."

Kirsty and Becky, who were listening, held their breath. Would the goblin fall for Rachel's trick?

Friends Forever

"Hmm," said the goblin.

Then he hopped across to the ledge, turned the bucket upside down and shook it over the ledge. Out tumbled three sweet wrappers, a cabbage leaf and a little pink box shaped like a heart. Rachel felt *her* heart leap with excitement, but she was careful not to show her feelings. The goblin plonked himself down beside the nearest rock pool and started scooping his net into the water.

Rachel looked up and caught Becky's eye.

"Now!" she whispered.

As fast as an
arrow, Becky
flew straight
towards the ledge
and put her
arms around
the trinket box.
It shrank to
fairy size as soon
as she touched it,
and she twirled into
the air, laughing with
joy and relief.

"Hey!" squawked another goblin,
pointing at her. "What's that fairy got in
her arms?"

The spottiest goblin had been busy
putting seaweed on his head, but he
turned and stared at Becky in horror.

"Give that back!" he screeched, leaping to his feet. "It's mine!"

"It most certainly is *not* yours," said Becky. "Jack Frost took it from me, so I have taken it back. You can tell him that I won't let him spoil any friendships."

The goblin's bottom lip started to wobble as the other goblins crowded around him, shaking their fists at the girls.

"But if I can't keep the trinket box safe, I'll never win Jack Frost's Best Friend Competition," he wailed miserably. "Give it back!"

Even though he was a naughty goblin, the girls didn't like to see him so upset. Kirsty came down from the boulder and put her arm around him. Rachel gave him her handkerchief.

"You can't have it back," she said in a gentle voice. "Jack Frost should teach you that it's very wrong to take things that don't belong to you."

"You've got it all wrong," he snapped. "Jack Frost is the best friend a goblin could wish for, because he knows how much fun it is to play tricks on pesky fairies and meddling human beings!"

He blew his nose with a loud trumpeting sound. The other goblins began to squabble, and the girls looked at each other.

"Let's get back to the caravans before our parents start worrying about us," said Kirsty. "I don't think the goblins are going to listen to us."

They made their way back to Sunsands beach and pulled on their shoes. Becky fluttered between them, her face alight with happiness.

"It's wonderful to have my trinket box back," she said. "Thank you for helping me – I wouldn't have known what to do without you!"

"You're welcome," said Rachel.

"Are you going to take it straight back to Fairyland now?" Kirsty asked.

55

"Yes," said Becky. "I have to make sure that it is safely locked away, and find out if there is any more news about Jack Frost."

"Come back soon," said Rachel. "We want to help you to find your other missing objects."

"And we also need to find out more about Jack Frost's Best Friend Competition," Kirsty added. "I don't like the sound of that!"

"I'll be back as soon as I can," said Becky.

She pirouetted upwards and disappeared in a flurry of magical sparkles.

Rachel and Kirsty let out long sighs of relief and smiled at each other.

"I'm sorry for arguing with you today," said Rachel.

"Me too," said Kirsty. "You're my best friend – I never want to fall out with you again."

They hugged one another and then started to walk together back to the caravan site. In the distance, they could see Kirsty's parents sitting outside their caravan. They waved, and Mr and Mrs Tate waved back.

"I hope that we can help Becky find her magical objects before tomorrow," said Rachel. "Otherwise our friendship pool party will be a disaster."

"We *will* find them," said Kirsty in a determined voice. "Best friends never let each other down!"

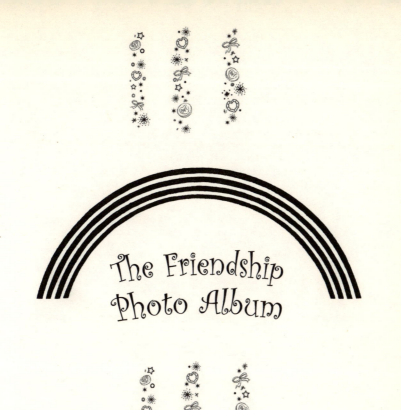

The Friendship Photo Album

Contents

Memory
Muddle

"Good morning!" called Kirsty Tate, putting her head around the caravan door.

Her best friend, Rachel Walker, was drawing at the table. She smiled when she saw Kirsty.

"Morning! How did you sleep?"

"Really well," said Kirsty. "Mum says that all the sea air makes us extra sleepy. The seagulls woke me up early though. They're better than an alarm clock!"

The girls and their families were staying at Sunsands Caravan Park for the whole weekend. Yesterday, their parents had told them that they were planning a paddling pool party to celebrate new friendships. They could invite whoever they liked. There were lots of other children staying at the caravan park, and Rachel and Kirsty had already started to get to know some of them.

"What are you drawing?" asked Kirsty, as Rachel made room for her on the caravan's bench seat.

"It's a picture of us together at the

paddling pool party," said Rachel.

Kirsty looked closely at the picture. Rachel had drawn a tree in the background, and something with tiny wings was just visible among the leaves. Kirsty smiled.

"Is that Becky the Best Friend Fairy?" she asked.

"Of course," said Rachel. "Our party wouldn't be complete without a fairy somewhere in the picture!"

The girls had been friends with the fairies for as long as they had known each other. They loved having magical adventures – even if things got a bit tricky sometimes!

"I hope that we can help Becky find the rest of her magical objects," said Rachel, putting her colouring pencil back in her pencil case. "We can't let Jack Frost make best friends fall out. There, I've finished my picture. What do you think?"

"It's really good," said Kirsty, looking at all the people and party food Rachel had drawn.

"I've drawn you eating your favourite party food," Rachel added. "It's the biggest bowl of jelly I could draw!"

But Kirsty frowned and her mouth trembled. Suddenly she felt all shaky inside.

"But my favourite party food is ice cream, not jelly," she said in a small voice. "How could you have forgotten that?"

Rachel put her hand over her mouth. "I'm really sorry. I just made a mistake."

"I would never forget any of your favourite things," Kirsty went on, feeling hurt. "I'm even planning to make the party theme your favourite colour – red."

"But my favourite colour is blue," said Rachel.

They girls stared at each other, feeling upset and confused. Then Rachel saw something out of the corner of her eye. She looked down and drew in her breath sharply. Her pencil case was glowing!

"That looks like magic," said Kirsty, instantly forgetting about being upset.

As the girls watched in excitement, the zip opened all by itself, and the glow became a bright sparkle.

Then Becky the Best Friend Fairy sprang out of the pencil case, smiling up at them.

"Hello, girls," she exclaimed. "I've come to take you to Fairyland!"

A Snowy Stadium

"I know where the friendship photo album is," said Becky, twirling around in her excitement. "Queen Titania looked in her Seeing Pool and saw what Jack Frost is doing today."

The girls loved the queen's Seeing Pool.

It was a magical place in the garden of the Fairyland Palace. When the queen waved her wand over the water, she could see things that had happened elsewhere, just like watching a film. "What did she see?" asked Rachel.

"Jack Frost is getting ready to hold his Best Friend Competition today," said Becky. "He's using my photo album to help him make up questions and challenges."

"Have you found out any more about the Best Friend competition?" asked Kirsty.

"All I know is
that he's looking
for a best friend,"
said Becky.
"Whoever wins
the competition
will be his new best
friend."

"What a strange way
to make friends," said
Rachel.

"Will you come with me?" Becky
pleaded. "I have to go to the
competition and try to get my photo
album back. I'm going to need some
help!"

"Of course we'll help," said Kirsty.

Just then, Rachel put her hand on
Kirsty's shoulder.

75

"I've just realised something," she said. "The friendship photo album helps best friends remember important facts about each other – right, Becky?"

Becky nodded, and Rachel looked into her best friend's eyes.

"That's why we forgot each other's favourite things," she said. "Don't be upset, Kirsty. It's all because Jack Frost has taken Becky's magical objects."

"You're right," said Kirsty, giving a relieved smile. "And that's another very good reason for us to get the photo album back as quickly as we can."

"Here we go!" said Becky.

She swished her wand, and a fountain of glittering fairy dust erupted from the tip. It sprinkled down on the girls and they started to shrink. Wings unfurled on their backs, and a few seconds later they were tiny fairies, just like Becky. Rachel and Kirsty fluttered upwards, delighted to be able to fly again, as Becky held up her wand.

"Three fairies need a magic way
To reach Jack Frost without delay.
Take us now, no time to lose!
For he has got a friend to choose.
This contest's strange, there is no doubt.
Let's save my album and get out!"

Fairy dust whirled around
them, faster and faster,
like a tornado of
sparkles. They were
lifted into the air
and the caravan
walls seemed
to melt away.
A rushing sound
filled their ears,
and then the fairy
dust stopped spinning.

They found themselves standing in the gardens of Jack Frost's Ice Castle, next to a gigantic white tent. A sign outside said: **Competition Stadium**.

"We're here," said Kirsty. "Jack Frost must be taking this competition very seriously. Come on, let's slip inside."

"What if we get caught?" asked Becky, looking nervous.

"Don't worry," said Rachel, giving her a confident smile. "We won't!"

The three fairies crept under the edge of the stadium tent and blinked. It was very dark inside and for a moment they couldn't see a thing. Then, as their eyes adjusted, Becky clutched Kirsty's arm in sudden panic. The stadium was filled with chairs, and there was a goblin on every single one. Some were clutching bags of crisps and others were slurping cans of pop. Cameras were flashing all over the stadium.

The fairies were standing at the side of the tent. At the front, a high stage had been set up, and several spotlights were shining on it. A long table faced the side of the stage, and Jack Frost was sitting behind it, side-on to the audience.

"Come on, let's hide behind one of the spotlights and see what's happening," Rachel suggested.

They flew upwards, unseen in the dim light, and tucked themselves behind the biggest spotlight. Just then, there was a blast of jangling music and three goblins shuffled onto the stage. Each of them was wearing a large, round badge with a number on it.

Jack Frost grabbed a microphone and turned to face the audience. The cameras flashed even more eagerly and the microphone squealed.

"Welcome to the semi-finals of my Best Friend Competition!" he roared.

Jack
the Judge

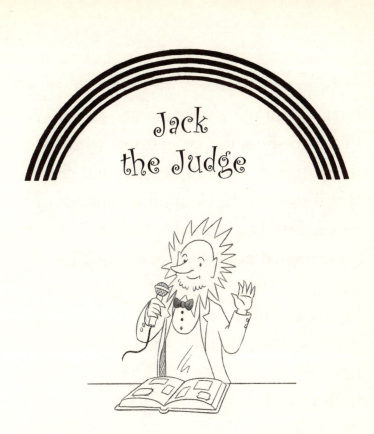

Jack Frost paused as if he was waiting
for something. Then he glared at the
audience.

"Applaud!" he hissed.

The goblins all clapped obediently and
Jack Frost held up his hands, smiling.

"No need, no need," he said. "Sit back, enjoy the performances, and don't forget to show the contestants what you think. If they do well, whistle and cheer. But if they make total nincompoops of themselves, boo and jeer. Got it?"

He turned back to face the goblins on the stage. They all looked very nervous. He looked down at a book that was lying open on the table in front of him, and turned a couple of pages. Then he looked up.

"First question goes to number one," he thundered.

"What would you do if I said something that you didn't agree with?"

Goblin number one nibbled his fingers for a moment and then said, "I would tell you that you were absolutely right."

"Excellent answer," said Jack Frost, as the audience burst into applause. "My next question is for goblin number two. What is my favourite perfume?"

"Ooh, I know this!" gabbled the second goblin. "Is it *Hint of Mould*?"

"Correct!" Jack Frost shouted over the sound of cheers and whistles. "The third question is for goblin number three. What is the name of the best band in the universe?"

The third goblin was squinting up at the spotlight where the fairies were hiding. They squeezed even further out of sight.

"I'm waiting!" Jack Frost screeched.

Goblin number two elbowed number three in the ribs.

"Oh, er, sorry," said number three. "I thought I saw…er…never mind."

"What's the answer, numbskull?" Jack Frost demanded.

Goblin number two whispered in number three's ear.

"The Angels?" said number three.

The stadium erupted with boos, laughs and jeers. Jack Frost bared his teeth.

"I have no idea how you made it this far," he said with a scowl. "I doubt very much that you will make it to the finals!"

Rachel and Kirsty were so interested in
the competition that for a moment they
forgot why they were there. But then
Becky gave a gasp.

"Look at the book in front of Jack
Frost," she said.

Rachel and Kirsty
could see that the
pages of the book
were covered in
photographs.

"Is that your
friendship photo
album?" asked Rachel in excitement.

Becky nodded, and Kirsty and Rachel
exchanged thrilled glances. They had
found it! But Becky did not look very
happy.

"How are we going to get it away

from him?" she asked. "It's out there in front of Jack Frost and a stadium full of goblins. We'll never be able to take it without being seen."

"Perhaps we don't have to worry about being seen," said Kirsty. "I've got an idea! Becky, can you turn us into judge goblins? If we can persuade Jack Frost to let us help him judge the competition, we can get the photo album while we're sitting at the table."

"Good thinking, Kirsty!" said Rachel. "Let's find somewhere to hide while we're transformed."

Jack Frost was still asking questions, and all eyes were on the contestants. No one noticed the three fairies swooping down behind a large speaker in the corner.

"Here goes!" said Becky, waving her wand.

Instantly, Rachel and Kirsty felt bumps and knobbles popping out all over their heads. Their skin turned bright green, and their noses grew long and hooked. They couldn't help but giggle as they turned into goblins. Kirsty was dressed in a silver suit, and her eyes were hidden behind dark sunglasses with a spiky pink rim. Rachel looked very peculiar in a mud-brown ballgown and a

neon-yellow tiara.

"You look horrible," said Kirsty, grinning at her best friend.

"You too," said Rachel, hugging her. "Perfect!"

"Good luck!" Becky whispered.

Treetop Challenge

Becky darted under a seat, from where she would be able to see everything. Then Rachel and Kirsty puffed out their chests and strode up to Jack Frost's judging table. His eyes opened very wide when he saw them and his mouth opened and closed silently for a few moments.

"Explain!" he croaked eventually.

"We're here to help," said Rachel. "Every head judge needs less important judges to boss around and shout at."

"And we can make sure that you don't miss a single thing the contestants do," Kirsty added. "Three pairs of eyes are better than one."

"Hmm, that's not a bad idea," said Jack Frost. "All right, you can be judges too. But I'm in charge!"

He sat down, and Kirsty took the
seat to his left. Rachel sat down on
his right. The friendship photo album
lay on the table in front of Jack Frost,
and he turned a few pages. He paused
when he reached some pictures of the
Party Fairies. Underneath the photos, in
golden letters, were the words:

*Best friends know each other's
favourite party food.*

Rachel and Kirsty exchanged a knowing glance. No wonder they had forgotten important details about each other earlier! Without the friendship photo album, the same thing would happen to best friends everywhere. They had to get it back.

"Next question!" said Jack Frost, his hand resting on the photo album. "What's my favourite party snack?"

"Coconut ice cream!" shouted goblin number one.

"Fizzy sweets!" number two yelled.

"Smelly socks!" cried the third goblin. "Wait, I might have heard the question wrong…"

"Idiot!" Jack Frost screeched. "Now, what shall I ask next?"

"Let me look through the book," said Rachel, reaching out to the album. "I'll find a good question."

But Jack Frost slapped her hand.

"It's mine, all mine!" he yelled. "I don't want slimy goblin hands all over it!"

Rachel rubbed her stinging hand, frowning. They would have to think of another way to get the album. Suddenly, an idea sprang into her mind.

"This is no way to choose a best friend," she said. "It's too easy to cheat. You have to find someone who will always stay by your side and help you

when you're in trouble."

"How am I supposed to do that?" Jack Frost demanded in a grumpy voice.

"How about hiding something that's precious to you?" Rachel suggested. "The first contestant to find it and bring it back to you will be the most helpful friend."

"That's a stupid idea," said Jack Frost, narrowing his eyes. "I've got a much better one. I'm going to hide something that's precious to me. The first contestant to find it and bring it back to me will be the most helpful friend."

Rachel hid a smile.

"What a wonderful idea," she said. "You're a genius."

"Of course I am," he snapped. "Now, what shall I hide?"

He looked around, and the girls crossed
their fingers under the table, hoping that
he would choose the photo album.

"This is the most precious thing in the
stadium," he announced, picking up the
photo album.

He marched out of the stadium tent
and crunched across the snowy lawn
towards a tall fir tree. Rachel and Kirsty
followed him at a distance, darting

behind ice-covered bushes whenever he looked around. When he reached the tree, he pulled out his wand and pointed it at the photo album. The album rose into the air, flapping its pages as if they were wings. As Rachel and Kirsty watched, the album nestled among the branches at the very top of the tree.

Then Jack Frost turned and retraced his steps.

"Now to tell those nincompoops what to do," he muttered as he strode back to the tent.

The girls jumped up.

"Where's Becky?" asked Kirsty. "She can just fly up to the top of the tree and get the book."

"Oh no!" said Rachel with a groan. "She must still be in the stadium! I bet she couldn't fly out without the goblins spotting her."

Kirsty and Rachel looked at each other worriedly.

There was only one way to reach the top of the tree. They were going to have to climb!

Climbing Contest

The girls rushed over to the tree and began to climb. But Kirsty's shiny suit made her slip on the branches, and Rachel's ballgown kept snagging on the bark. They hadn't climbed very high when they heard voices shouting below. The three goblin contestants were racing towards them across the snow.

"Stop!"

"Cheats!"

"You're judges – you can't compete!"

The goblins scrabbled up behind
the girls, climbing swiftly. Number
two grabbed a handful of Rachel's
ballgown and tugged, making her slide
downwards. He clambered over her.

"Quick!" called Rachel to her best
friend. "You can do it!"

Kirsty was almost at the top, but goblin number one reached up his hand and grabbed her ankle, holding her back.

"No!" she cried as he tried to push her aside.

She shook off his hand and pulled herself up, stretching out her fingers to the album. As she grabbed it, she saw Becky zooming out of the stadium towards the tree.

"Give that to me!" squawked goblin number one.

As he tried to wrestle the book out of her hand, he shoved Kirsty backwards and her suit slipped on the branch where she was sitting. Still clutching the book, she tumbled out of the tree!

"Kirsty!" cried Rachel.

But a sparkling shaft of magic shot from Becky's wand, and both girls were changed back into fairies again. They fluttered up into the grey skies above the Ice Castle. Below, they could see Jack Frost shaking his fist and jumping up and down in fury.

110

"We did it!" cried Kirsty as Becky flew up to join them.

Becky took the book and a dazzling smile lit up her face. The three fairy friends hugged in mid-air, twirling around like snowflakes.

"Thank you a million times over!" Becky said. "But now I must send you home and take the photo album back where it belongs."

111

"Will we see you again soon?" Rachel asked.

"Of course you will," said Becky. "We have to find the BFF charm before your party this afternoon!"

They broke apart and Becky flicked her wand. As they blinked, the Ice Castle vanished and they found themselves back in Rachel's caravan. No time had passed since Becky had flown out of Rachel's pencil case.

"What an exciting adventure!" said Kirsty.

Something thumped against the side of the caravan, and the girls got up and went outside. Two little boys were playing with a ball.

"Sorry," called one of the boys. "It was an accident."

"No problem," said Kirsty. "We love playing ball too. Can we join in?"

"Sure," said the boy with a grin. "I'm Jim and this is my best friend Theo."

The girls introduced themselves and started to play. Jim and Theo were great fun.

"We should invite them to the party this afternoon," said Rachel as she kicked the ball to Kirsty. "It's so much fun making new friends."

"Good idea," Kirsty replied. "We just have to hope that we can find the BFF charm in time!"

The BFF Charm

Contents

A Spy
at Sunsands

Kirsty was humming to herself as she
made preparations for the pool party.
She was feeling excited about it, and
hoping that she and Rachel would be
able to get Becky's BFF charm back
from Jack Frost before it started.

Mr Walker had already set up the
paddling pool, and it was Kirsty's job to
arrange the chairs around it. Rachel had

gone to fetch some tables. Kirsty put the final chair in place and looked around. Rachel was nowhere in sight, but a girl was pulling a table along, with her back to Kirsty.

"Excuse me, have you seen my friend?" Kirsty asked.

The girl stood up and turned around. To Kirsty's astonishment, she saw that it was Rachel!

"Didn't you recognise me from behind?" Rachel asked, sounding upset.

"I thought you'd know me anywhere."

Kirsty felt very upset too, but she took a deep breath and remembered what Becky had told them.

"This isn't happening because I don't know you," she said, squeezing Rachel's hand. "It's all because Jack Frost still has the BFF charm. Becky said that its power makes sure best friends recognise each other anywhere. We have to help her get it back before the pool party, or else everyone's best friends will get mixed up."

"I hope we see Becky again soon," said Rachel. "It's horrible to think that I might not recognise you!"

The girls finished setting up the tables and smiled at each other as Mr Walker walked around the side of the caravan, pulling a hose.

"Time to start filling the pool for the party!" he said. "I hope you've invited lots of new friends to splash around with you."

"We've made six new friends," said Rachel, counting them off on her fingers. "We met Kitty and Elsie yesterday – they like stamp collecting."

"And we met Theo and Jim this morning," Kirsty added. "They were great fun!"

"There's a little girl called Alice

staying in the caravan next door to us with her best friend, Naomi," Rachel added. "I met them earlier and invited them too."

"We've met a few new friends too," said Mr Walker. "I think we'll all have fun getting to know them better."

He aimed the hose at the pool and turned it on. The girls squealed as a blast of water spattered into the pool and sprinkled them with cool droplets.

Laughing, Mr Walker turned the pressure down.

"Could you go and fetch the pool toys from the car, girls?" he asked.

"Ooh yes, I forgot about the toys!" Rachel exclaimed. "We've got loads of fun things to play with. Come on, Kirsty."

Together, the best friends skipped around to the other side of the caravan. Just as they rounded the corner, Rachel stopped and clutched Kirsty's arm.

"Did you see that?" she asked.

"See what?" Kirsty replied.

"I'm sure I just glimpsed someone
ducking down behind our car," Rachel
said. "Quick – let's see who it was!"

The girls raced around to the other
side of the car, but there was no one to
be seen.

"Perhaps you were mistaken," said
Kirsty.

"Maybe," said Rachel, shrugging her
shoulders. "I'm sure I saw *something*,
though. Oh well, let's get the pool toys
and take them back to Dad."

They filled their arms with floats,
goggles, water pistols and balls, and
staggered back around the caravan
to drop them into the pool. Then Mrs
Walker leaned out of the caravan
window.

127

"If you've finished out there, could you come and help me with the food?" she called. "I want to make sure that there's plenty to go around."

Soon Kirsty was busily icing cupcakes, while Rachel filled bowls with crisps, nuts and vegetable sticks. Kirsty had just done a swirl of pink icing on the last

cake when she glanced up and gasped.
Someone was peeping through the
caravan window!

A Safe Secret

"Stop!" Kirsty cried.

She dashed out of the caravan and saw a figure darting around the corner of the next caravan. Rachel raced up behind her.

"There *was* someone watching us!" Kirsty exclaimed. "They've gone around that caravan, and I know it's a dead end. They must be waiting there for us."

"Maybe it's Becky," said Rachel, her heart thumping with excitement. "Perhaps she wants to lead us somewhere hidden, where she can talk to us without being seen."

"It didn't look like Becky," said Kirsty in a doubtful voice. "But I suppose she might have been in disguise. Whoever it was, we have to find out why they're watching us. Come on!"

They hurried around the corner of the caravan, but no one was there. The girls stopped, puzzled.

"There's nowhere else for them to have gone," said Rachel.

Kirsty had an idea.

"There is *one* place," she said.

She crouched down and peered into the dark space under the caravan. Then she gasped and scrambled to her feet.

"What is it?" asked Rachel. "*Who* is it?"

"You'll never guess," said Kirsty in a breathless voice.

There was a scrabbling noise, and then someone crawled out from the space under the caravan, covered in mud and sand. Rachel gasped and took a step backwards.

"*Jack Frost!*" she exclaimed.

Jack Frost stood up and brushed the mud and sand off his cloak. He looked cross, as usual, but he also looked a little bit embarrassed.

"Nosy humans," he muttered.

"Why are you following us and spying

on us?" Kirsty demanded.

Jack Frost looked down at the ground and shuffled from side to side. The girls looked down too, but saw nothing. He cleared his throat and looked up at the sky. Rachel and Kirsty looked up too, but there was nothing to see.

"What are you looking for?" Kirsty asked, feeling curious.

"Oh, all right!" he snapped. "I was watching you to get ideas for questions to ask in the final of my Best Friend Competition."

"Why did you think *we* could give you ideas?" asked Rachel.

Jack Frost scowled. "Because you're best friends, OK? Because you're actually a little bit…well…you're quite good at it. At being friends."

His cheeks flushed a darker shade of blue, and he looked even more cross than usual. Rachel and Kirsty exchanged puzzled glances and Jack Frost bared his teeth.

"All right!" he snarled. "Your friendship is the best one I've ever seen. I want a friend like that! The goblin who wins my competition will get my friendship, as well as a special BFF charm, so the decision I make has to be right."

"You have to give the charm back to Becky," said Kirsty at once. "It's not right to keep something that doesn't belong to you."

"Don't be silly," said Jack Frost. "She'll never get it back. It's locked in my safe until the final of the competition. Then

136

it will belong to my best friend! So stop bleating about right and wrong, and tell me some good best friend questions!"

"No, we won't," said Rachel, folding her arms.

Jack Frost stamped his foot.

"Fine!" he shouted. "I'll think of some questions all by myself. And they'll be five million times better than anything your puny human brains could come up with!"

There was a blue flash, a loud thunderclap, and Jack Frost vanished.

Locket Magic

Rachel and Kirsty stared at each other
in astonishment.

"We have to tell Becky about the
safe," said Kirsty, putting her hand to
the locket around her neck.

Rachel did the same. The lockets were
a gift from Queen Titania, and they
contained magical fairy dust to carry the
girls to Fairyland.

"Ready?" asked Rachel.

"Ready," said Kirsty.

At the same time, they opened their lockets and sprinkled the fairy dust over each other.

"Take us to Becky!" said Rachel in a clear voice.

Magical sparkles danced around them, and they watched each other as they shrank to fairy size and gossamer wings appeared on their backs. When they were no taller than the blades of grass around them, a warm breeze puffed and lifted them up into the air. They whirled

around, with fairy dust glimmering
before their eyes. When it faded, they
were standing outside a little white house
with a painted rainbow
arching above the
front door. Kirsty
stepped forward
and knocked on
the door. It opened
almost at once, and
Becky stood there
smiling at them.

"Welcome to my
home," she said.

"Oh, Becky! We've found
out where the BFF charm is!" Rachel
gasped. "Jack Frost is keeping it in his
safe and he's going to give it to the
winner of his competition."

Becky's hands flew to her mouth.

"How can we get it out of the safe?" she asked.

"We can't," said Kirsty. "The only way to open a safe is to know the secret code, and I'm sure Jack Frost won't tell it to us."

"Then whatever am I going to do?" Becky asked with a groan. "Without the BFF charm, people and fairies will stop knowing who their best friends are."

"I've been thinking," said Rachel suddenly. "There's only one thing we *can* do. The winning contestant gets the charm, right?"

"Right," said Kirsty and Becky together.

"Then it's simple," said Rachel. "One of *us* has to win the competition!"

Becky looked alarmed, but Kirsty's eyes lit up.

"You're right!" she exclaimed. "But can we do it?"

"Of course," said Rachel, hoping that she sounded confident. "All we need is a bit of magic and courage!"

"First we have to get to the competition," said Becky. "Come on – there's no time to lose!"

143

She pulled her front door shut and zoomed up into the blue sky. Rachel and Kirsty followed close behind her, taking a moment to gaze at the lush green hills and pretty toadstool houses all around them.

"Fairyland is so beautiful," said Kirsty. "I'm sorry we can't stop and look around. I love it here!"

"Me too," said Rachel. "But right now we have to get to the Ice Castle before the competition starts."

Flying at top speed, the three fairies soon reached the forest that separated Fairyland from Jack Frost's gloomy Ice Castle. Here, the sky was full of grey clouds, and a biting wind made everyone shiver. They flew over the snow-topped trees until they saw the castle's battlements. Several goblin guards were marching up and down on duty.

"Look!" said Kirsty, pointing at a huge white tent in the gardens. "That's the competition stadium. I bet Jack Frost is holding the finals in there."

Rachel, Kirsty and Becky flew over to the tent and slipped inside.

A Fake at
the Final

The stadium was even more packed
than the first time the fairies had been
there. There were goblins on chairs,
goblins standing in the aisles and goblins
crammed in the doorways. They were
eating, drinking and making such a
racket that the fairies couldn't hear each
other speak.

Becky pointed to the long table in front of the stage. Once again, Jack Frost was sitting there with his back to the audience. Rachel cupped her hand over Becky's ear and spoke in a loud voice.

"The contestants aren't on the stage yet," she said. "Can you turn me into a goblin? I've got an idea!"

Becky waved her wand, and instantly Rachel felt bumps bulging up on her head and face. Her nose grew long and her feet spread wide and turned green.

A few seconds later, her fairy wings had disappeared and she looked exactly like a goblin.

"We have to get backstage," she said in a squawky voice.

She stomped down the side of the stadium tent, and Becky and Kirsty flew up to the ceiling and fluttered above her. Rachel scampered up the steps to the stage and then slipped backstage. Two goblins were pacing nervously up and down. A tall, skinny goblin was wearing a badge saying "1", and a shorter, plumper goblin was wearing a badge saying "2".

"We have to get one of them away from the competition," Becky told Kirsty. "Then Rachel can take his place. But how?"

"Food," said Kirsty in a confident voice. "That's the quickest way to distract a goblin."

Becky's eyes twinkled, and then she waved her wand. Instantly, a large box appeared at the side of the stage, filled to the brim with green cupcakes. The plump goblin was busily reading a list of Jack Frost's favourite smells, but the skinny goblin saw the cakes at once. His eyes popped and he scurried towards them.

With a flick of Becky's wand, the box slipped out of sight around a corner. The goblin followed it, and Becky flicked her wand again.

"That box will lead him all the way to the other side of the Ice Castle," she said. "By the time he's finished eating the cakes, the competition will be over."

Just then, the jangling music that signalled the start of the competition rang in their ears. Quickly, Becky used her magic to give Rachel a big '1' badge. Then the plump goblin grabbed Rachel and hissed, "Come on!" He dragged her out onto the stage where they stood under a blazing spotlight. The competition had begun!

"About time!" shrieked Jack Frost's voice.

Rachel couldn't see anything because the spotlight was shining into her eyes, but Becky and Kirsty could see Jack Frost sitting at the table and scowling at the two contestants.

"We're about to find out who's a pal and who's pathetic," he declared. "Who's my buddy and who's a bad apple. Welcome to the finals of my Best Friend Competition!"

The crowd went wild, lights flashed around the stadium and the loud music shook the ground.

"Just say whatever you think Jack Frost will want to hear," Rachel muttered to herself. "You have to win this competition!"

"Question one," said Jack Frost. "What is a best friend's most important job?"

"Shining your shoes?" asked the plump goblin.

"Anything you say it is," said Rachel.

"Question two," Jack Frost went on. "Why do you want to be my best friend?"

"Because it would be so cool!" the plump goblin said in a squeaky voice.

"Because you're the most amazing, handsome, incredible person in the human and fairy worlds," said Rachel.

She didn't dare to look up. She was
sure that she would giggle if she caught
Kirsty's eye when she was giving these
silly answers!

"And the final
question," said
Jack Frost.
"What is
the best
thing
about
me?"

"Your
hair," said
the plump
goblin.

"It's impossible to decide," said Rachel.
"Everything about you is so totally
fantastic!"

Drums rolled and the whole stadium went dark. Two small spotlights picked out Rachel and the other goblin. Which one would Jack Frost choose?

A Worthy Winner

"I have made my decision," Jack Frost's voice boomed out of the darkness. "The winner is...*goblin number one!*"

The crowd cheered and clapped, glittering ice-blue confetti showered down on Rachel, and Jack Frost marched up the stage. Two goblins pushed a safe forward to the middle of the stage.

"As my new best friend, you will wear my BFF charm at all times," Jack Frost declared.

He tapped the secret code into the safe and the door swung open. Inside, the BFF charm glinted under the dazzling lights.

"You are the winner!" Jack Frost boomed.

He picked up the charm and placed it on a long chain. Then he put the chain around Rachel's neck.

Instantly, Becky waved her wand and Rachel was transformed into a fairy again. A gasp went up from the crowd.

"Cheat!" the goblins squawked. "It's a pesky fairy! Fraud! Double-crosser!"

Rachel put her hands on her hips and looked Jack Frost in the eye.

"You took the BFF charm from Becky," she said. "Now I can give it back."

Becky and Kirsty zoomed over to Rachel and hugged her. The confetti was still tumbling around them. Rachel took off the charm necklace and handed it to Becky. Then they all turned to face Jack Frost.

They were expecting him to be
jumping up and down in fury, but he
was silent. His shoulders slumped and he
sat down on the edge of the stage.

"I should never have bothered," the
fairies heard him mutter. "No one really
wants to be my friend anyway."

He put his head in his hands and
Kirsty took a step forward. Rachel bit
her lip, and Becky raised her wand.

They all wanted to make him feel better. But before Becky could use her best-friend magic, someone pushed past her. It was the plump goblin who had been the other finalist. He was carrying a glass of

water, and the fairies watched him hand Jack Frost the drink.

"How are you, Your Iciness?" he asked.

Jack Frost took the water and looked up at the goblin. Then something amazing happened. Jack Frost smiled! Becky smiled too.

"My magic isn't needed here after all," she whispered. "Sometimes, friendship is magic enough. Come on – it's time for me to send you home to the human world."

She tapped their lockets with her wand, and they filled with fairy dust once

more. Then she put her arms around them both.

"One of the most wonderful things

about being the Best Friend Fairy is that there is always something new to learn about friendship," she said. "You two have shown me how powerful true friendship can be. Thank you."

"It was so much fun!" said Rachel.

They all hugged each other, and then

the stadium and the goblins vanished in a swirl of glittering fairy dust. Seconds later, Rachel and Kirsty were back at Sunsands, close to Rachel's caravan.

"Rachel! Kirsty!" they heard Mrs
Walker calling. "Your guests are here!"

The girls ran around the caravan.
Kitty, Elsie, Jim, Theo, Alice and Naomi
were already splashing in the pool,
laughing together. Rachel and Kirsty
shared a happy smile.

"It looks as if friendships are back to normal," said Rachel.

"And even Jack Frost won a friend after all," Kirsty added. "Best friends really are *amazing!*"

Now it's time for Kirsty and Rachel to help...

Elle
the Thumbelina Fairy

Read on for a sneak peek...

Rachel Walker skipped along the riverside path, enjoying the warmth of the sun and the scent of flowers in the air. Her best friend, Kirsty Tate, did a cartwheel beside her and laughed. It was always exciting to spend a weekend together, but this weekend was going to be extra special. They were going to the Wetherbury Storytelling Festival, and they could hardly wait.

"Hurry up, Mum!" called Kirsty, looking back along the path. "It's almost time!"

Their favourite author, Alana Yarn, was going to be sharing her best storytelling tips, and the girls were really looking forward to seeing her.

"Don't worry, we won't be late," said Mrs Tate with a smile. "Look, the festival tents are just up ahead. Besides, my cartwheeling days are over, Kirsty."

"I'm never going to stop doing cartwheels, even when I'm grown up," said Kirsty.

She grinned at Rachel.

They reached the bright festival tents, which were decorated with bunting and huge book pages.

"They look as if they come from a giant's book," said Rachel in delight.

"I do miss getting lost in storybook worlds," said Mrs Tate. "The books I loved best as a child were filled with imaginary things like magic and fairies."

Kirsty and Rachel exchanged a smile. They knew that fairies were real, not imaginary! In fact they had lots of fairy friends, but they were the only two people who knew about it.

"Oh look!" Kirsty exclaimed.

She pointed to where a boat was moored by the riverbank. There was a sign on the path beside it, saying 'Story Barge', and the boat itself was piled high with books. A man was standing on the barge, smiling at them.

"Are you here to see Alana Yarn?" he called.

The girls nodded, and Mrs Tate smiled.

"Have fun, both of you," she said. "I'll see you later."

She hugged them goodbye and then

they skipped over to the Story Barge.

"Welcome to the Storytelling Festival," the man said. "Alana Yarn is about to start. Go and sit over there, in the grassy hollow. She won't be long!"

Rachel and Kirsty hurried over to where a large group of children was sitting on cushions.

They were in a circle around a bench, which was shaped like a book. There weren't very many empty cushions left, but the girls found two next to each other and sat down.

"I feel as if I might burst, I'm so excited!" said Rachel.

"Me too," Kirsty replied. "I can't believe that Alana Yarn is actually going to be here!"

They had read all Alana Yarn's books, and had even queued up in bookshops when a new one came out. The other children in the group looked thrilled too.

"She's here!" someone exclaimed.

Heads bobbed and necks craned as everyone tried to see the famous author. Rachel and Kirsty glimpsed a mane of curly black hair. Then Alana Yarn took her seat on the book-bench, and smiled around at her audience. She had a wide, warm smile and sparkling blue eyes with thick, black lashes.

Read **Elle the Thumbelina Fairy** to find out what adventures are in store for Kirsty and Rachel!

RAINBOW magic ®

Join in the magic online by signing up
to the Rainbow Magic fan club!

Meet the fairies, play games and
get sneak peeks at the latest books!

There's fairy fun for everyone at

www.rainbowmagicbooks.co.uk

You'll find great activities, competitions, stories and
fairy profiles, and also a special newsletter.

Find a fairy with
your name!